Series 401
A Ladybird Book

MR. BADGER TO THE RESCUE is an exciting story, told in verse, about three little Dormice who have many adventures before Mr. Badger comes to their rescue and takes them to the circus.

MR. BADGER
TO THE RESCUE

Story and illustrations by A. J. MACGREGOR

Verses by W. PERRING

Publishers: Ladybird Books Ltd . Loughborough
© Ladybird Books Ltd (formerly Wills & Hepworth Ltd) 1949
Printed in England

Once upon a Monday morning,
    When the sun was rising red,
Little Mousies wakened, startled,
    Sat up suddenly in bed !

"What a noise !" said Sister Tilly,
    "Let us take a look outside !"
Out they scrambled, to the window :
    "Well !" they said : and "Oo" they
                              cried.

4

0 7214 0315 8

There, below them, through the woodland,
　　Came a circus, out of town!
Scarlet-collared geese for horses,
　　At the fore, a Monkey-Clown!

Birds and bunnies, woodland mousies
　　Gazed and gazed with sparkling eyes,
Clapping, running, most excited
　　At this wonderful surprise!

Eager Mousies looked for money—

    They must pay to see the show.

. . . Bag and money-box were empty,

    Pockets too ! They couldn't go !

Tilly wept and Tommy sniffled,
    Tiny Timmy wiped his eye:
And, when Monkey-Clown came knocking,
    Woeful Mousies breathed a sigh.

Told him that they had no money,
    Showed him empty pockets too:
Monkey-Clown said " Why not earn it? "
    And they wondered what to do.

So they went to Mr. Squirrel,

    Asked if he could see a way:

" Why not fetch the woodland washing?

    Woodland folk will gladly pay ! "

Off they went with Tiny's barrow

Straight to Mrs. Porky Pry.

Tommy knocked, but Mrs. Porky

Chased him off without reply !

Down the lane ran sorry Mousies,

    Reached the fence of Mrs. Hare :

Wondered, was she in the garden ?

    Looked to see if she was there.

Mrs. Hare was pulling turnips,

Digging carrots with her fork:

Mousies thought she might be working

Much too hard to stop and talk.

Rather timidly they called her :

   Mrs. Hare obeyed the call,

Listened kindly : then she answered,

   " But your barrow is so small ! "

Sorrowfully Mousies left her :

   Now they'd *never* see the show !

Never get inside the circus !

   Every one had answered " No ! "

Then they saw the sign-post pointing

    Up to Mr. Badger's house.

" Shall we try *him*, Tom ? " said Tilly,

    " Do you think *he'd* help a mouse ? "

" Oh, we might as well ! " said Tommy,

    " For it isn't far to go."

So they went to Mr. Badger,

    Told him all about the show.

" Why, of course ! " said Mr. Badger,

" Come with me, I'll put you right ! "

When they got *two* extra barrows,

Mousies twittered with delight.

Off they hurried for the washing,

By the tents, and Monkey-Clown;

Off to Mrs. Bunny's cottage,

Right across the Woodland Town!

Here they found the washing flapping,

　Nearly ready, in the breeze.

Mrs. Bunny had her clothes line

　Tied across between the trees.

Soon she had it piled in baskets,

    Packed each barrow with its load,

And, at last, the eager Mousies

    All were ready for the road.

But, before she let them leave her,

Mrs. Bunny said " Take care !

For the road is very bumpy :

When you reach the bridge, beware ! "

Up the hill and down the hollow,

    To the bridge across the stream!

Tilly, leading, struck a boulder!

    Tilly gave a little scream!

Over went poor Tilly's barrow!
   Over went poor Tilly, too!
Over went the washing basket,
   To the river down below!

Frog held up his hands in horror!
   Tommy's barrow ran away—
Tommy tried to miss poor Tilly,
   But 'twas their unlucky day!

Tommy down and Tilly injured!

    Everything was going wrong!

Meanwhile, what about the washing,

    Sailing merrily along?

Mr. Frog had seen their trouble,
  Seen the washing basket go,
Went and told the tale to Badger,
  Fishing down the stream below.

Mr. Badger hadn't seen them,
  For the bridge was out of sight:
So he packed his things and hurried—
  He could help them in their plight!

As he crossed the bridge he saw them,

    Sad of face upon the brink,

Trying hard to reach the basket:

    Called out " Stop, you'll make it sink ! "

Tiny heard him, waved and shouted:

Badger hastened to their aid:

Waded in and got the basket,

Safe, but soaking, I'm afraid.

When they saw the dripping washing,
    Mousies stared in great dismay :
Mr. Badger packed it for them,
    Wheeled the barrow all the way.

" Oh dear, what will Mrs. Hare say ? "
    Mousies said as they drew near.
Mrs. Hare was *very* troubled,
    Said " Oh dear, oh dear, OH DEAR ! "

Though the washing soon was mangled,
    Soon put out once more to dry,
Yet the Mousies still had nothing,
    And they all began to cry.

Mr. Badger wiped his glasses,
    Said " Well! Well! Just as I feared!
Never mind, my dears, I'll take you! "
    How the Mousies clapped and cheered!

Off they hurried to the circus,
    Mr. Badger paid the clown.
And, inside, some seats were empty,
    At the front. They all sat down.

How they clapped the clever sea-lion,
    With the ball upon his nose!
How they cheered and laughed and chattered
    At this glorious show of shows!

Happy, happy little Mousies,
    With their more than happy friend.
Glad that he had brought their troubles
    To this very happy END.